DOSE OF DECEPTION
COLE STEELE

ONE

Lori Tolliver stood in front of the building she had just leased for her fledgling law practice, staring up at the sign that read "Tolliver Law." It was a small, run-down building in a part of town that had seen better days, but it was all she could afford.

Lori had just finished law school, graduating from Belmont University and was eager to start her own practice. She had always been driven and independent, and the idea of working for someone else had never appealed to her. But now that she was standing in front of her new office, she couldn't help but feel a little intimidated.

The building was old and musty, with peeling paint and cracked windows. The hallway leading to Lori's office was dimly lit, and she could hear the faint sound of dripping water coming from the floor's only bathroom.

As she unlocked the door to her office, she couldn't help but feel a sense of pride. This was her space, her chance to make a name for herself. She had always known that starting a law practice would be a challenge, but she was determined to make it work.

Lori walked into her new office and looked around. It was a small room, with just enough space for a desk, a few chairs, and a filing cabinet. She had bought a used desk and chairs, and the walls were bare except for a few law books she had brought from home.

She sat down at her desk and took a deep breath. She had no clients yet, no cases to work on, and barely enough money to pay the rent. But she was determined to make this work.

As she was lost in thought, she heard a knock at the door. She got up and opened it to find her brother Shaun standing outside.

"Hey sis," he said, grinning at her. "Need some help setting up?"

Shaun had just been released from prison after serving a five-year sentence for assault. He was looking for a job, and Lori had decided to hire him as her private investigator. She knew it was a risk, but she also knew that he was smart and resourceful, and she trusted him. Shaun had taken it upon himself to defend his sister from a stalker when the authorities ignored her pleas for help.

"Sure, thanks," she said, stepping aside to let him in.

Together, they spent the afternoon setting up her office, organizing files, and discussing strategy. Lori told Shaun about her plans to focus on legal cases involving pharmaceutical companies and medical malpractice.

As they worked, Lori couldn't help but feel a sense of excitement. This had been her dream ever since the first mock trial she had participated in during high school. And now with Shaun by her side, she knew that anything was possible.

But as the day wore on, Lori couldn't shake the feeling that something was off. The building was too quiet, too empty. It was like they were the only ones there. That shouldn't have been a surprise though given the area and low cost of the rent.

TWO

Lori woke up early on a rainy morning, eager to start working on her new practice. She made herself a cup of coffee and settled in at her desk, listening to the rain tapping against the windowpane.

As she checked her email, her phone rang. It was a woman named Sarah Murray.

"Ms. Tolliver, I'm sorry to bother you so early, but I need your help," Sarah said, her voice shaking.

Lori could hear the desperation in Sarah's voice, and she felt a sense of urgency to help her. "Of course, Sarah. What's going on?"

Sarah explained that she had recently given birth to a baby boy and had been given a drug during the C-section that she believed may have caused some adverse side effects. She was now unable to care for her baby, and she was in danger of losing custody of him. She didn't know what to do, and she had found Lori's new advertisement online. Sarah explained that she had talked to another firm but didn't sound interested and referred her to some ambulance chaser named Darwin Kent. Lori told Sarah she saw one of the man's commercials the other night and knew of him.

Lori listened to Sarah intently. She could hear the desperation in her voice during their conversation. She told Sarah to come to her office that afternoon, and they would discuss things further.

As Lori waited for Sarah, she watched the rain pour down outside, the streets slick and wet. A fast-flowing current in the gutter collecting everything in its way taking them toward the storm drain. She hoped Sarah would be able to make it to her office safely.

When Sarah arrived, Lori was struck by how frail and exhausted she looked. She was clearly struggling, and Lori could see the fear in her eyes.

Lori invited Sarah into her office and offered her a seat. "Tell me everything, Sarah. I want to help you," Lori said, leaning forward.

Sarah told Lori her story, taking breaks to catch her breath. She explained how she felt the drug had caused damage to her nervous system, leaving it difficult to care for her baby. Sarah had been to a couple of neurologists, but they were either unable or reluctant to point toward the IV she had been given during her C-section. She had no family to turn to for help, and she was at risk of losing her child to the state.

Lori listened intently, taking notes on a yellow legal pad as Sarah spoke. She could see how much this child meant to her.

"I'll take your case, Sarah. I promise you that I will fight for you and your child," Lori said, placing a reassuring hand on Sarah's arm.

As Sarah left the office, Lori watched as she made her way out into the rain, huddled under an umbrella. She felt a pang of worry for her client, hoping she would be able to make it home safely.

THREE

A pleasant cool breeze whistled through an opening in the slightly cracked window. It had taken a nearly herculean effort to free the damn thing as it appeared to have been hastily painted shut. The smell of mold lingered, but the cramped workspace was simply going to have to do.

Suddenly, there was a knock at her door. Lori got up to answer it, and when she opened it, there stood Mitchell Payne, Shaun's parole officer. He was a tall man with a crew cut and a stern expression. He looked like he could go from zero to asshole in a split second.

"Hello, Ms. Tolliver," he said, stepping into the office.

"Officer," Lori replied, gesturing for him to take a seat.

As they sat down, Payne explained that he was there to check on Shaun's employment status. Lori told him that Shaun was working for her now as a private investigator.

Payne sounded surprised. "Really?" But I still need to make sure he's not using. And, Shaun, I'm going to need you to provide a sample."

Shaun's stood at the door with his arms folded. He had hoped to avoid the exercise altogether. Every once in a while, there was an urge to use a vape pen to relax.

"Of course," Lori said quickly. "Shaun, you can use the restroom down the hall."

Payne followed Shaun to the bathroom and stood outside the door while he provided the sample. It was an awkward situation, and it reminded Shaun of how little privacy there was in prison.

When Shaun emerged, Payne took the sample and examined it closely before sealing it in a plastic bag.

"Everything looks good," Payne said, handing Shaun a business card. His new parolee quipped "Here I was worried about dehydration. Glad it was so clear." Payne cleared his throat. "Call me if you have any questions or concerns. And keep an eye on him if you would, Ms. Tolliver."

With that, Payne left the office, and Lori breathed a sigh of relief. She was glad that Shaun's employment status was approved, but she couldn't help feeling sorry for him. Parole was a tough road, and she knew that Shaun was doing everything he could to stay on the straight and narrow. The judge in his case had been recently elected at the time of Shaun's sentencing and had made an example out of him for political purposes.

FOUR

Lori had made them both sandwiches for lunch, trying to cut costs wherever she could because her fledgling practice hadn't generated any income.

Shaun took a bite of his turkey sandwich with a light spread of yellowy mustard and then looked at Lori with concern. "When do you think we'll start making some money? I mean, I appreciate you hiring me and all, but I don't want to be a burden."

Lori sighed, "I know, Shaun. Trust me, I know what you're thinking. We need this hold on Sarah's check to clear the bank, and then we'll finally have our first paying client. Until then, we'll have to make do with what we have."

Shaun nodded, "I get it. It's just hard being unemployed for so long, and now I feel like I'm not contributing enough."

"I couldn't do this without you."

Shaun smiled, "Thanks, sis. I appreciate that."

Just then, her cellphone chimed, interrupting their lunch. Lori picked it up and swiped the screen with her thumb. She turned to Shaun with a bit of nervous excitement.

"That was my bank. We finally have our first paying client!"

Shaun grinned, "That's great news! Maybe we can finally afford to eat something other than sandwiches."

Lori looked down at her plate, "Let's not get ahead of ourselves, but at least we'll be able to pay the rent this month."

FIVE

The next morning, Lori sat down at her desk, picked up the phone and called the hospital's medical records department. After being on hold for several minutes, a clerk finally answered.

"Hello, this is attorney Lori Tolliver," Lori said. "I'm calling on behalf of my client, Sarah Johnson. She's been trying to obtain her medical records from you but appears to be having some difficulty."

The clerk on the other end of the line listened patiently as Lori explained the situation. When Lori was finished, the male sighed heavily and said, "I'm sorry, but we can't release her records yet. They're incomplete."

"Incomplete? How can that be? Sarah gave birth months ago."

"I understand your frustration, but there are some missing records that we need to track down. We'll release them as soon as we can." the clerk explained.

Lori could sense that she wasn't going to get anywhere with him, so she decided to take a different approach. She hung up the phone and called Sarah to let her know what had happened.

"I'm sorry, Sarah, but it looks like the hospital is being difficult," Lori said when Sarah answered the phone. "They're saying that your records are incomplete and that they can't release them yet."

Sarah let out a frustrated sigh. "I tried to get them once before, and they told me the same thing. How can they be incomplete? What's taking so long?"

"I don't know, but I'll keep pushing them," Lori promised. "In the meantime, let me see if there's anything else we can do to move your case forward."

Lori hung up the phone and leaned back in her chair, deep in thought. She knew that they couldn't wait around for the hospital to release the records. They needed to find another way to get the information they needed.

As she sat there, the phone rang, interrupting her thoughts. It was Sarah, and she sounded panicked.

"Lori, I just got served with a summons for unpaid medical bills. What am I going to do?" Sarah said, her voice trembling.

Lori knew that this was going to complicate things even further. She took a deep breath and said, "Don't worry. We'll figure it out. Let me make a few calls."

SIX

Lori slammed the phone down in frustration. She had just gotten off the line with the hospital's medical records department for the second time, and they still had not released Sarah's complete medical history. It was like pulling teeth trying to get them to cooperate.

Shaun looked over at her from his desk, concern etched on his face. "What's going on?"

Lori stood up and walked over to her window. "They're still claiming that Sarah's medical records are incomplete. I asked them if it had anything to do with her unpaid medical bills, and they wouldn't say. But I have a feeling that's what's going on."

Shaun frowned. "Can they do that? Hold her medical records hostage like that?"

Lori shook her head. "No, and it's not ethical. They must know it hinders my ability to properly represent her. Maybe they were instructed to try and wait it out hoping our client runs out of money and we go away."

Shaun nodded in agreement. "What are you going to do?"

Lori leaned back in her chair, thinking. "I'm going to call them back and tell them that if Sarah's complete medical history isn't delivered to our office in the next 24 hours, we will subpoena the hospital. It's a strong-arm tactic, but we don't have time to waste. Sarah needs our help now."

Shaun nodded, impressed. "I like it. Let's show them we mean business."

Lori grabbed the phone and dialed the hospital's number again. After a few minutes of being put on hold, she finally got through to someone. She explained the situation, and when she didn't get the response she wanted, she made her intentions clear.

"Between my client and I we've made reasonable attempts to procure her medical history." Lori said firmly.

There was a pause on the other end of the line, and Lori could hear the person typing something. "I understand your concern, Ms. Tolliver. Let me see what I can do."

SEVEN

Lori sat at her desk, surrounded by stacks of legal textbooks. She had been researching civil court procedures for hours, trying to ensure that she was fully prepared for what would follow after her summons and complaint was filed.

She glanced out the window at the bustling street below, watching as people hurried by in the late afternoon sun. She loved living above the bistro, with the smells of fresh bread and coffee wafting up to her apartment, but it could also be noisy at times.

As she continued her research, she couldn't help but worry about the lack of progress on Sarah's case. She had made some headway with the hospital, but the issue of the missing medical records was still unresolved.

Lori knew she needed to stay focused, though. She couldn't let her concerns about Sarah's case distract her from her studies. She took a deep breath and refocused her attention on the legal text in front of her.

After a while, she leaned back in her chair and stretched her arms above her head. It was late, and she knew she needed to get some rest. She closed her textbooks and turned off her laptop, feeling a sense of satisfaction at the progress she had made.

As she crawled into bed, she couldn't help but wonder what the next day would bring. Would the hospital finally turn over Sarah's medical records? Would she be able to move forward?

She tried to push those thoughts out of her mind and closed her eyes, letting the sounds of the bistro below lull her into a peaceful sleep.

EIGHT

The next morning, Lori woke up to find a courier standing at her door holding a package. She quickly signed for it and eagerly tore it open, revealing Sarah's complete medical history.

Relief washed over Lori as she pored over the documents, finally having the full picture of what possibly had happened to Sarah. She could now move forward with the case, armed with the evidence she needed to prove that Sarah's medical condition was a direct result of the medication she had been given during her c-section.

While she read through the documents, there was a knock at the door. It was the landlord's maintenance team, there to fix the leaky faucet in her apartment bathroom. Lori had been so focused that she had forgotten to follow up with the landlord about the repair request.

She let the maintenance team in and showed them the bathroom, grateful that the issue would finally be resolved. The constant dripping between home and office was close to torture. As they worked, Lori couldn't help but think about how she had been struggling to make ends meet, barely able to afford her rent and office lease.

As the maintenance team finished up and left, Lori settled back into her research, feeling a renewed sense of determination.

NINE

Lori reviewed Sarah's medical history and then discovered a pattern of C-section deliveries that all had used the same drug called "*Eferidine*." She had never heard of this drug before and decided to do some research. After several hours of searching online medical journals and databases, Lori finally found some information about *Eferidine*. It was a relatively new drug, manufactured by Kemper Pharmaceuticals out of New Brunswick, New Jersey. It was primarily used to control shivering during epidural anesthesia, which was commonly used during C-section deliveries. Lori couldn't help but wonder if there was a connection between the drug and Sarah's debilitation. She made a mental note to do more research on the potential side effects of *Eferidine* and to contact a medical expert to learn more. The next day, Lori was back in her office, ready to dive deeper into the research on *Eferidine*. She had set up a meeting with a local medical expert, Dr. Patel, to discuss her findings and get his opinion. Lori couldn't believe it. It seemed like every time she uncovered a piece of information, it only led to more questions. She decided to shift her focus back to the *Eferidine* research. She printed out all of the articles she had found and headed to her meeting with Dr. Patel. He was a kind and knowledgeable man who had been practicing family medicine for over thirty years and had delivered plenty of newborns. Lori explained her findings and showed him the research she had collected on *Eferidine*. Dr. Patel listened intently and then asked to see Sarah's medical records. After reviewing them, he confirmed that *Eferidine* had been used during her C-section delivery. He also noted that there had been reports of side effects, including muscle weakness, chronic lethargy, and nerve damage, which could explain Sarah's current debilitation.

Lori was stunned. She had a strong suspicion that the drug was the culprit behind Sarah's condition, but hearing Dr. Patel's confirmation made her heart sink. She knew that this news would be devastating for Sarah.

Dr. Patel continued to explain that Kemper Pharmaceuticals had received multiple reports of adverse reactions to *Eferidine*, but they had failed to notify the FDA or issue a recall. Instead, they continued to market the drug to hospitals and healthcare providers.

TEN

Lori knew that she needed more information to determine if there was a connection between *Eferidine* and Sarah's debilitation, and the only way to do that was to investigate the one case she had found against Kemper Pharmaceuticals.

She sent Shaun to New York to interview the plaintiff, Ms. Anderson, and try to uncover any information he could about the case. However, Shaun was on parole and not allowed to leave the state. Lori understood the risk and explained it to him. He didn't bat an eye at his sister's request after she had given him the news.

After a few days of investigating, Shaun was able to locate the Plaintiff in the New York case, a woman by the last name of Anderson, and scheduled an interview. During their conversation, Ms. Anderson revealed that her attorney had filed a motion for Summary Disposition early on in the case, which led to the case being dismissed almost immediately. She suspected that her attorney had taken a bribe from Kemper Pharmaceuticals to tank the case after immediately consulting with another law firm soon after.

Shaun also learned that Ms. Anderson had suffered from muscle weakness and nerve damage, similar to Sarah's condition, after receiving *Eferidine* during her C-section delivery.

Shaun reported back to Lori with his findings, and Lori knew that they needed to act fast before any more victims fell through the cracks. The clock was certainly their greatest enemy at the moment.

ELEVEN

Lori spent the next few weeks preparing the lawsuit against Kemper Pharmaceuticals. She carefully drafted the complaint, outlining the details of Sarah's medical history and the potential link between her debilitation and the use of *Eferidine* during her C-section delivery.

Lori had decided to file the suit in Davidson County Circuit Court, located in the heart of Nashville. She felt confident in the local court system and believed that it would be more advantageous to keep the case closer to home.

Once the complaint was finalized and filed, Lori's next plan was to get Kemper Pharmaceuticals served with the lawsuit. She knew that serving a large corporation could be a challenge, especially one located out of state, but she was determined to make it happen.

Lori had done her research and found a recent Supreme Court case that furthered her confidence in the lawsuit. The case had ruled that a drug manufacturer could be sued even after the FDA had given its blessing for approval. This meant that Lori's case could proceed, even though *Eferidine* had been approved by the FDA.

With a favorable Supreme Court ruling, Lori felt much more confident. She contacted a local process server and provided them with the necessary paperwork to serve Kemper Pharmaceuticals.

TWELVE

Lori Tolliver could feel her pulse moving a little more rapidly. The judge looked stern and imposing behind his bench, and she could see Kemper's attorneys in the corner of her eye whispering amongst themselves and writing on yellow legal pads.

The judge began by asking Lori to present her case, and she did her best to articulate the argument she had developed over the past few weeks. She emphasized the potential side effects of *Eferidine* and the pattern she had observed in Sarah's medical history, as well as the fact that the Supreme Court had recently ruled that drug manufacturers could be sued even after FDA approval.

Kemper's attorneys argued that the case should be dismissed because Sarah's medical records did not definitively link her debilitation to the use of *Eferidine* during her C-section delivery. They also claimed that the lawsuit was frivolous and lacked merit.

Lori stood her ground and passionately argued her case, pointing out the potential harm that could be caused by allowing pharmaceutical companies to escape liability for their products.

After hearing both sides, the judge took a brief recess to review the evidence and make a decision. Lori was on pins and needles, unsure of what the ruling would be.

When the judge returned, he announced that he was denying Kemper's motion to dismiss the case. Lori felt a surge of relief and excitement. Her case was going to trial.

THIRTEEN

Her client's health had been deteriorating and the stress of an impending trial was not helping matters. Lori wanted to do everything in her power to make the process as easy as possible for Sarah.

"Lori, thank you for letting me know," Sarah said, her voice weak. "I trust you to handle everything, but I don't know about a deposition. I'm not feeling well, and the thought of going through that is making me anxious."

She knew how stressful legal proceedings could be, and with Sarah's health in decline, it was essential to keep her stress levels as low as possible.

Lori decided to reach out to a colleague of hers, Dr. Franklin, who was a specialist in stress management techniques. She explained Sarah's situation and asked for any advice or resources that might help her.

Dr. Franklin listened intently and then recommended a few techniques that might be beneficial, such as deep breathing exercises, meditation, and guided imagery. He also provided some resources for support groups and counseling services.

Lori thanked him for his help and immediately passed the information along to Sarah, who was grateful for the additional support.

"I will be there every step of the way to make sure you are comfortable and supported. Your health is my top priority."

Sarah sighed, relief washing over her. "Thank you, Lori. I don't know what I would do without you. You've been a true blessing in all of this."

Lori smiled, grateful for the trust and appreciation from her client. "I promise, we will get through this together."

FOURTEEN

Lori spent the next few days researching court reporters in the area. She knew that the costs could add up quickly, and she wanted to make sure she was getting the best value for her client.

She reached out to colleagues for recommendations and scoured online reviews to narrow down her options. After careful consideration, she settled on a court reporting firm that had a reputation for being reliable and efficient.

Lori called the court reporting firm and spoke with a representative who provided her with a quote for their services. The representative explained that their fees were based on a per-page rate, which included the transcription and any necessary formatting. Lori asked for details about the experience of the court reporters and whether they had worked on cases similar to hers. The representative assured her that they had a team of experienced reporters who had covered a wide range of cases, including pharmaceutical litigation.

Despite the challenges and stress of the legal battle, Lori remained determined and focused. She was committed to fighting for her client's rights and holding Kemper Pharmaceuticals accountable for their actions.

FIFTEEN

It was troubling to hear that his parole officer had paid him a surprise visit and searched his apartment. Lori knew that her brother Shaun was trying to turn his life around and this kind of interference from Payne could make things difficult for him.

"Are you okay, Shaun?" Lori asked, concern in her voice.

"Yeah, I'm fine," Shaun said, his voice a little shaky. "I just didn't know how to explain to him where I had been. And then he started searching my place, tearing everything apart. I didn't know what to do."

Lori listened attentively, trying to come up with a solution. "Did he find anything?"

"No, there's nothing there. But he did seem suspicious when I couldn't provide an alibi for my whereabouts."

Lori frowned, thinking hard. "Shaun, there may be something else going on here. Remember when you were in New York? You mentioned that you thought someone went through your belongings in the hotel room."

Shaun thought for a moment before answering. "Now that you mention it, I did feel like someone had gone through my things. My bag was open, and some of my clothes were on the floor."

"That's a good lead," Lori said, her mind racing. "We can try to get surveillance footage from the hotel and see if anyone entered your room during the time you were there. It's a long shot, but it's worth a try."

"Do you think it was intentional? Who would just look through my things without taking something, it's sort of creepy." said Shaun. Did this happen before or after your visit to see Ms. Anderson?" asked Lori. Shaun paused for a moment. "It was after, I had gone outside to a street vendor to get something to eat because someone had me on a budget, not to name names or anything."

"You missed my sandwiches, didn't you? " asked Lori.

"Definitely cuisine compared to the food in prison."

Lori chuckled. "I'll chalk that one up as a compliment."

SIXTEEN

Sarah was in a state of panic as she dialed Lori's number. When Lori picked up, Sarah's voice was shaking. "Lori, I think my tires were slashed this morning," she said. "I went to take out the trash and noticed my front tire was completely flat. Then I checked the opposite rear tire, and it was flat too."

Lori could hear the fear in Sarah's voice. "Did you see or hear anything suspicious?" she asked.

"No," Sarah replied. "The baby was asleep, and I had just enough energy to get something done around the house."

Lori thought for a moment before asking, "Do you have any sort of wireless surveillance like a camera pointing out toward the street?"

"No, I don't," Sarah said. "I never thought I would need one."

Lori replied, "Now might be the time to invest in it. Call the police and make a report so this is documented. I will send Shaun over to help you with the flat tires."

Shaun, who was sitting beside Lori, looked at her curiously. "What was that all about?" he asked.

"I don't know just yet," Lori replied. "But we need to make sure Sarah is safe and secure."

SEVENTEEN

Sarah's mind raced as she tried to think of a reason why someone would do this to her car. She had never had any issues with anyone before and couldn't understand why someone would want to cause her trouble.

Shaun could see the worry etched on Sarah's face and knew he had to do something to help. He assessed the situation and realized there was only one spare tire, which meant Sarah's car would need to be towed to a tire store.

"I know it's tough, Sarah, but don't worry. We'll get this sorted out," said Shaun reassuringly.

Sarah nodded and handed him her keys. "Thank you so much for your help. I don't know what I would do without you and Lori."

Shaun got in touch with the tow truck driver and rode along to the tire store with him. Once they arrived, Shaun explained the situation to the staff and asked if they had any used tires, they could sell them. Luckily, they had a good selection that would work for Sarah's car.

Shaun quickly called Sarah to let her know the good news. "They have some used ones that will work perfectly for your car. You can pay over the phone with your debit card once the repairs are finished."

Sarah breathed a sigh of relief. "Thank you so much, Shaun. I don't know what I would do without you."

Shaun smiled on the other end of the line. "I'm just glad I could help."

After the tire repairs were done, Shaun drove the car back to Sarah's house. She thanked him profusely for his help.

As they walked to her front door, Shaun said, "You might want to look at some wireless cameras online. They're usually fairly inexpensive and might give you some peace of mind."

Sarah nodded thoughtfully. "You're right, I never thought about getting a camera before. But now that this has happened, I don't want to take any chances. I'll look into it and see what options are available."

Shaun gave her a reassuring smile. "It's always better to be safe than sorry. And with a camera, you can keep an eye on your car and your home from anywhere."

Sarah felt a sense of relief at the thought of having extra security measures in place. She promised to do some research and find a reliable camera system to install.

EIGHTEEN

Lori and Shaun exchanged a curious glance after a knock on the open office door, then turned their attention to a man standing in there in the hall. "I'm looking for attorney Tolliver. I was driving back from a friend's house last night and I got pulled over by the cops," he explained. "They said I was driving erratically and suspected me of driving under the influence. I was given a breathalyzer test and said I was over the legal limit, but I only had a couple of beers. I don't think it was accurate." "I see," said Lori, nodding thoughtfully. "Well, I can certainly help you with that. Do you have any paperwork or documentation from the police?" The man handed over a small stack of papers, and Lori skimmed through them quickly. "It looks like your car was impounded because you refused to take a blood or urine test. That's something we can discuss further, but for now, let's focus on getting your car back. Do you have the capacity to pay a retainer fee at this moment? I'd like to take on your case." The man pulled out his wallet and took out a credit card. Lori reached into her desk drawer and grabbed a couple pieces of paper. "I just need some information from you." Shaun pulled out his phone and started searching for impound lots in the area. "There are a few options nearby.

We can call to see which one has your car and arrange for a release."

The man nodded gratefully, and Lori started filling out the necessary forms on her computer while Shaun made the phone calls. As they worked, the man explained more about what happened the previous night, insisting that he wasn't driving under the influence.

"I waited a while before leaving to make sure I was okay to drive," he said. "I even had some food to absorb the alcohol. But when the cops pulled me over, they were really aggressive and kept insisting that I was drunk. I guess I got nervous and refused the blood and urine tests."

Lori listened intently, making notes on a legal pad as the man spoke. "Okay, let's talk about your options," she said.

"First, we need to get your car released from impound. After that, we can start building a defense strategy. We can request a hearing to challenge the license suspension. And we can also request discovery from the prosecutor's office to get more information about their case against you."

The man looked relieved to have a plan of action, and Lori continued to explain the legal process as Shaun worked on arranging for the car's release. After a few more phone calls, he finally found the impound lot where the car was being held and arranged for the release.

With the car situation taken care of, Lori turned her attention back to the man's case. "Let's schedule a follow-up meeting to go over the details and discuss your options," she said. "In the meantime, I suggest you avoid any alcohol or drugs and be cautious when driving to avoid any further legal troubles."

The man thanked Lori and Shaun for their help, and they watched him leave the office closing the door behind him.

NINETEEN

Lori smiled as Shaun walked in, glad for the distraction from the stress of the pharmaceutical litigation case. "Hey, Shaun. Take a seat," she said, gesturing to the chairs in front of her desk.

Shaun dropped his backpack onto one of the chairs and settled in. "So, what's the latest with the car impoundment case?"

Lori leaned forward and picked up a file from her desk. "I may have something going with that already. I spoke with one of the assistant prosecutors, and we might be able to work out a plea deal."

Shaun raised an eyebrow. "Really? Do you think the guy will take it? I mean, he sounded pretty adamant that there wasn't any alcohol in his system."

Lori nodded. "It's always hard to say, but I think we have a good chance. We'll argue that it's more of a procedure issue now. Did the police do exactly what they were supposed to when they tested him after the stop? Was the breathalyzer calibrated? Were their certifications up to date before using it? That sort of thing."

Shaun nodded thoughtfully. "Makes sense. I hope it works out for him."

"What's that beeping sound? That an alarm on your phone or something?" Shaun felt his phone in his pocket, "no, why?" "Listen, I hear that, don't you?" said Lori. Shaun got up from his seat, but the noise was coming from directly next to him inside his backpack. "What the hell?" Lori looked at her phone. "It says there's an unregistered device nearby." Shaun had the same message on his phone. "Mine too." Shaun dug through his backpack pulling everything out and placing it on Lori's desk. She moved some things out of the way to make room. "I still hear it, now whatever that is sounds like a bird chirping." Shaun shook his backpack upside down and an AirTag tumbled out then bounced on

Lori's desk and hit the floor where it started to roll toward the heating vent. Shaun scrambled after it and retrieved the thing before it could've been lost forever. He held it up in the palm of his hand for both of them to examine. "You know what this is?" asked Shaun. "I think so, you can use it to find your keys or anything you might misplace." said Lori. Shaun put it down on Lori's desk. "Sometimes it's used to track people, the only way we knew it was here because our phones and their signals are relaying its position right now." "Looks like you picked up a stow away between here and New York." said Lori. "Probably from the hotel room. My clothes strewn about were the distraction." "Well, someone is certainly interested in what you were doing out there." said Lori.

TWENTY

Lori breathed in the rich aroma of the bistro's kitchen as she waited for her food to arrive. The smell of garlic and herbs mixed with the sound of sizzling from the grill. She was pleased with herself for securing her second client and decided to treat herself to a small dinner.

As she waited, the waiter returned with an unexpected message. Her bill was being picked up by a man at the end of the bar who wanted to speak with her. Lori leaned to the side to see him, and the waiter pulled up another chair for the man to sit across from her.

"May I?" he asked, gesturing to the seat across from her.

"Sure," Lori replied, trying to keep her cool.

The man sat down and made himself comfortable with his drink. "I'm Gerard Beckham and my firm represents Kemper Pharmaceuticals."

Lori felt her pulse quicken from a bit of nervousness, but she tried to keep her composure. "Thought I recognized you from the motion hearing the other day. Something keeping you here in Nashville?"

Beckham set both of his hands on the table. "That's why I wanted to speak with you."

Lori quipped, "My contact information was on the complaint."

Beckham dismissed her remark. "I understand you have the best interest of your client at heart. The gung-ho idealism to right every wrong and seek justice in a seemingly unfair world."

Lori pretended to sound stunned. "Wow, can't even imagine why I even went through law school and passed the Bar Exam to run smack into this type of reality."

Beckham took a drink from his glass half filled with bourbon. "Belmont University, I believe if I'm not mistaken."

Lori eyed him suspiciously. "There some kind of dossier on me back at the firm?"

Beckham studied his glass for a moment as some condensation slid down its side. "Only what was relevant."

Lori waited for the waiter to set her food down and walk away after making sure everything was to her liking. "I was worried there for a minute, I thought you might resort to something lower like tracking my movements."

Her blood went cold after Beckham spoke. "Parole violations in some states can be tricky, especially if a prosecutor and judge are both up for re-election."

"That a threat?" asked Lori.

"I don't have any use for threats, Ms. Tolliver. Your brother Shaun worked hard in prison to keep his nose clean and get out early. It'd be a shame for him to have to go back inside."

Lori Tolliver's voice turned serious. "That sounded like a threat. I think we're done here."

Beckham stood up and slowly pushed his chair toward the table. "My client is willing to negotiate without admission of any wrongdoing if you drop the suit. Kemper is willing to fly you and your client out to discuss the terms."

Lori looked around the Bistro. "Actually, I'm quite comfortable here. But I do want one thing though."

Beckham finished his drink. "I'm listening."

Lori looked up at him and smiled. "Make sure your client is on time for their deposition."

TWENTY-ONE

The cellphone on Lori's kitchen counter chimed several times before she had a chance to answer it. Sarah had been rushed to the hospital after falling at home. A co-worker was kind enough to take care of the baby for the interim. Lori called Shaun right away. "Meet me at the hospital." Shaun quickly replied. "What happened? Are you okay?" Lori responded. "It's not me, it's Sarah." Shaun let his sister know he could be there in about ten minutes.

They met in the parking lot and walked in together stopping at the information desk close to a bank of elevators. When they arrived at Sarah's room, she was sitting up in bed looking at her phone. A nurse followed in behind them and checked Sarah's blood pressure. "I thought I was tired before, they don't let you rest in here at all." Lori surveyed the room and noticed her client was connected to a lot of monitors. "What happened?" My baby was crying so I got up to see what was the matter. When I took a step, my legs simply gave out underneath me. I crashed to the floor but managed to get to the couch and call 911. "How do you feel now?" asked Lori. Sarah's legs moved under the thin white sheet and matching hospital blanket. "I can move my feet and everything. They ran a bunch of tests." Lori looked back out in the hallway which was heavy with foot traffic from the hospital staff moving about. "Let's talk with your neurologist and see what they have to say." Sarah nodded slowly then looked out her room's window.

Lori and Shaun were back in the elevator heading down toward the lobby. "What do you think?" asked Shaun. Lori felt the elevator car slow to a stop then watched the doors part. "Certainly feels connected to *Eferidine* and her case."

Lori and Shaun stepped out of the elevator and into the busy hospital lobby. They made their way to the neurology department and met with Sarah's neurologist, Dr. Peters. Dr. Peters went over the test results with them, pointing out that Sarah's symptoms were consistent with peripheral neuropathy, a condition that affects the nerves and can cause weakness, numbness, and pain in the hands and feet.

Lori asked if there was any connection between Sarah's condition and the medication she had been given after her C-section. Dr. Peters nodded and confirmed that *Eferidine*, the drug in question, had been known to cause peripheral neuropathy in some patients.

TWENTY-TWO

Lori sat across from the CEO of Kemper Pharmaceuticals, Barry Scott, in the virtual office she had leased in downtown Nashville. She had never seen him in person before, but she had seen pictures and videos of him online. He was a tall man with slicked-back silver hair and piercing blue eyes. He wore an expensive suit and a watch that probably cost more than Lori's car.

Gerard Beckham, the company's attorney, sat at Scott's side, his beady eyes watching Lori closely.

Lori took a deep breath before beginning her deposition. "Mr. Scott, can you confirm that Kemper Pharmaceuticals manufactures the drug *Eferidine*?"

Scott nodded, his eyes never leaving Lori's. "Yes, we do."

"And can you confirm that *Eferidine* has been linked to cases of peripheral neuropathy?" Lori asked.

Scott hesitated for a moment before answering, "Yes, there have been some cases reported."

Lori leaned forward, studying Scott's face for any signs of discomfort. "So, you knew that *Eferidine* could cause peripheral neuropathy?"

Scott remained calm, "We were aware of the potential side effects, yes."

Lori raised an eyebrow, "And yet, Kemper Pharmaceuticals failed to warn patients like my client, Sarah, about the risks associated with the drug?"

Scott's jaw tightened, "We believed that the benefits of the drug outweighed the risks."

Lori leaned back in her chair, "But my client is now suffering from nerve damage as a result of taking *Eferidine*. How do you justify that?"

Scott looked down at his hands before responding, "We take the safety of our patients very seriously, Ms. Tolliver. We are constantly monitoring our products and their side effects and make adjustments as necessary."

Lori studied Scott's face, looking for any signs of deception. "Yet, you didn't make any adjustments in the case of *Eferidine* until after Sarah and others like her were harmed."

Scott's eyes narrowed, "We did what we thought was best at the time."

Lori shook her head, "But it wasn't best for Sarah, was it?"

Scott's face remained impassive, "We regret any harm that our products may have caused, but we stand by our decisions."

Lori felt a wave of anger wash over her. This man was responsible for so much suffering, yet he sat there with a smug look on his face, defending his company's actions.

After the deposition ended, Lori watched Scott and Beckham gather their things and leave. She felt a sense of frustration and anger, but also a renewed determination to fight for justice for her client and all those who had been harmed by Kemper Pharmaceuticals' negligence.

TWENTY-THREE

She checked her phone and saw that she had missed several calls from Shaun. She dialed him back, "Hey, what's up?"

"I found something interesting," Shaun said. "I spoke to a former employee of Kemper Pharmaceuticals who claims that they knew about the risks associated with Eferidine but chose to ignore them."

Lori's ears perked up, "Really? Who is this person?"

"Her name is Maria Martinez. She worked in the clinical trials division and said that she raised concerns about the side effects of Eferidine, but her boss told her to keep quiet."

Lori felt a sense of excitement. This could be the smoking gun they needed to prove that Kemper Pharmaceuticals was negligent. "Can you set up a meeting with her?"

"I already have. She's willing to talk to us," Shaun replied.

"Great, let's meet her tomorrow," Lori said.

The next day, Lori and Shaun met with Maria Martinez at a coffee shop in downtown Nashville. Martinez was a middle-aged woman with short brown hair and a stern expression.

"Ms. Martinez, thank you for meeting with us," Lori said.

Martinez nodded, "I want to do the right thing. I know that people have been hurt by Eferidine, and I can't just sit by and do nothing."

Lori leaned forward, "Can you tell us more about what you know?"

Martinez took a deep breath, "I was working on the clinical trials for Eferidine, and I noticed that several patients were reporting symptoms of peripheral neuropathy. I brought this up to my boss, but he told me to keep quiet and not to worry about it."

Lori's eyes widened, "And who was your boss?"

Martinez hesitated for a moment before answering, "His name was David Schmidt. He was in charge of the clinical trials division."

Lori jotted down the name in her notebook. "Thank you, Ms. Martinez. This information is incredibly helpful."

Martinez nodded, "I just want to make things right. I hope that you can get justice for those who have been harmed."

Lori and Shaun left the coffee shop, feeling energized. They had a new lead and a potential witness who could help them build their case against Kemper Pharmaceuticals.

As they walked down the street, Lori turned to Shaun, "Let's track down David Schmidt and see what he has to say."

Shaun nodded, "I'm on it."

TWENTY-FOUR

Lori and Shaun spent the next few days tracking down David Schmidt, the former head of Kemper Pharmaceuticals' clinical trials division. They finally located him living in a retirement home in a nearby town.

They arranged a meeting with him, and Lori and Shaun arrived at the home, not sure what to expect.

Schmidt was a thin, frail-looking man with white hair and a deeply lined face. He was sitting in a wheelchair, staring out the window when Lori and Shaun walked in.

"Mr. Schmidt, thank you for meeting with us," Lori said.

Schmidt turned to look at them, his eyes dull and lifeless. "What do you want?"

Lori took a deep breath, "We're investigating the side effects of Eferidine and the role that Kemper Pharmaceuticals played in failing to warn patients. We understand that you were in charge of the clinical trials division."

Schmidt snorted, "I don't know anything about that."

Lori leaned forward, "We have reason to believe that you were aware of the risks associated with Eferidine and chose to ignore them."

Schmidt looked away, "I did what I was told. I had orders from the top."

Lori felt a wave of anger wash over her. This man was responsible for so much suffering, yet he was trying to shift the blame onto others.

"Who gave you those orders?" Shaun asked.

Schmidt hesitated before answering, "Barry Scott. He knew what was going on, but he didn't want anyone to know. He said that the drug was too important to the company's bottom line."

Lori felt a sense of satisfaction. They finally had the smoking gun they needed to prove that Kemper Pharmaceuticals was negligent. "Thank you, Mr. Schmidt. This information is incredibly helpful."

Schmidt shrugged, "It doesn't matter. I'm an old man. What difference does it make?"

Lori and Shaun left the retirement home, feeling a mix of emotions. They had what they needed to prove that Kemper Pharmaceuticals had knowingly put patients at risk, but at what cost?

As they drove back to Nashville, Lori thought about all the people who had been harmed by Eferidine. She was determined to get justice for them, no matter how hard the fight.

"We're getting close," Shaun said, breaking the silence.

Lori nodded, "Yeah, we are. But we still have a long way to go."

TWENTY-FIVE

Lori and Shaun walked out of an office supply store with some newfound confidence. They were both exhausted but knew they still had work to do.

As they were putting things in the trunk, Lori's phone rang. She answered it, "Hello?"

"Ms. Tolliver, this is the retirement home where David Schmidt was staying. I'm sorry to inform you that he passed away last night."

Lori felt a sense of sadness wash over her. They had lost a key witness in their case against Kemper Pharmaceuticals.

"Thank you for letting me know," Lori said, before ending the call.

Shaun looked at Lori, "What are we going to do now?"

Lori sighed, "We'll have to find another way to prove our case. We still have the evidence, but without Schmidt's testimony, it's going to be harder to convince a jury."

As they arrived back at the office, Lori couldn't help but feel frustrated.

Shaun immediately tried to call Maria Martinez, the former Kemper Pharmaceuticals employee who had provided them with valuable information. But her phone had been disconnected.

Lori felt a sense of disappointment. They had lost another key witness in their case. "We'll have to keep looking," she said.

Over the next few weeks, Lori and Shaun continued their investigation, trying to find new leads and gather more evidence. But it seemed like every door they knocked on was closed.

Lori felt a sense of frustration with her first case. She couldn't help but think about all the people who had been harmed by Eferidine and how they deserved justice.

One night, as she was poring over documents in her office, Lori's phone rang. She answered it, "Hello?"

"Ms. Tolliver, this is Maria Martinez."

Lori felt a sense of relief wash over her. "Maria, where have you been? We've been trying to reach you."

"I had to go into hiding. I received some threats after I spoke to you and Shaun," Martinez said.

Lori's eyes widened, "What kind of threats?"

"They told me to keep quiet or else," Martinez said.

Lori felt a sense of anger wash over her. How could someone be so heartless as to threaten someone who was trying to do the right thing?

"Maria, we need you to testify at the appeal," Lori said.

Martinez hesitated before answering, "I don't know. It's too risky."

Lori took a deep breath, "Maria, we need your help. We're fighting for justice here. We can't let Kemper Pharmaceuticals get away with what they did."

Martinez was silent for a moment before finally saying, "Okay. I'll do it."

Lori felt a sense of gratitude wash over her. They still had a chance to fight.

TWENTY-SIX

The door to her office was cracked open slightly. Lori thought Shaun had arrived to get an early start. There were times that he had mentioned his inability to sleep during the night, his thoughts going back to being incarcerated.

Lori pushed the door open and discovered that her office had been ransacked. Her pulse quickened, Lori quickly checked to make sure there was no one still lurking around.

As she surveyed the damage, Lori felt a sense of anger wash over her. How could someone be so heartless as to destroy her office and try to intimidate her into dropping the case?

She took a deep breath and tried to calm herself down. She knew she needed to focus on the case and not let the stranger get the best of her.

But as she started to clean up the mess, Lori couldn't shake the feeling that she was being watched. She felt like the stranger was lurking in the shadows, waiting to strike again.

Suddenly, the phone rang, jolting Lori out of her thoughts. She picked it up, her voice shaky. "Hello?"

"Lori, it's Shaun," came the voice at the other end. "Are you okay? I just got a text from you saying that the office has been ransacked again."

Lori felt a sense of relief wash over her. She was grateful to have Shaun by her side, even if it was just over the phone.

"I'm okay," Lori said, her voice steadier now. "I'll fill you in when you get here."

As she hung up the phone, Lori noticed something out of the corner of her eye. There was a piece of paper on the floor that hadn't been there before. She picked it up and read the message.

"We warned you to stop. Next time, it won't just be your office."

Lori's hands shook as she read the message. She knew that she was in real danger now, and that she needed to take extra precautions.

When Shaun arrived at the office a short while later, Lori showed him the message. Shaun's eyes narrowed as he read it.

"We need to take this to the police," Shaun said, his voice determined.

Lori hesitated for a moment. She didn't want to involve the police, but she knew that Shaun was right. They needed to take action before it was too late.

Together, they went to the police station and filed a report. The officers promised to increase patrols in the area and to keep an eye out for any suspicious activity.

TWENTY-SEVEN

As the trial drew closer, Lori and Shaun received disturbing news. Maria Martinez, their key witness, was becoming increasingly reluctant to testify. She had received threats in the past, but now she was more scared than ever.

Lori and Shaun decided to pay Maria a visit at her home. They found her sitting on the couch, her face etched with worry.

"Maria, what's going on?" Lori asked.

"I can't do it," Maria said, her voice shaking. "I'm sorry, but I can't testify. I've received more threats, and I'm afraid for my life."

Lori felt a sense of frustration wash over her. They had worked so hard to build their case, and now their star witness was backing out at the last minute.

"Maria, we need you," Shaun said. "Without your testimony, we don't have a case."

"I know, but I can't do it," Maria said, tears streaming down her face. "I'm sorry."

Lori and Shaun exchanged worried glances. They knew they had to do something to convince Maria to testify.

"Can you show us the messages you've been receiving?" Lori asked.

Maria hesitated for a moment before nodding. She handed over her cellphone, and Lori and Shaun started scrolling through the messages.

There were several messages from an unknown number, all of them threatening and menacing. But what was more alarming were the pictures. They were photos of Maria driving and at the grocery store, completely unaware that she had been photographed.

Lori felt a sense of anger wash over her. Someone had been watching Maria, and they were willing to do anything to stop her from testifying.

"We need to take this to the police," Lori said, her voice determined.

Maria shook her head. "No, I can't involve the police. They won't be able to protect me."

"Then we'll protect you," Shaun said. "We'll make sure you're safe."

Lori nodded in agreement. "Shaun's right. We'll do whatever it takes to make sure you're protected. But you have to testify. You have to help us bring Kemper Pharmaceuticals to justice."

Maria looked at Lori and Shaun, her eyes filled with fear and uncertainty. But after a few moments, she nodded. "Okay."

Lori and Shaun felt a sense of relief wash over them. They knew that the road ahead would be tough, but they were ready to face it head on. They would do whatever it took to make sure justice was served.

TWENTY-EIGHT

Lori and Shaun knew that they had to take Maria's concerns over her personal safety seriously. They couldn't risk anything happening to her before the trial. After much discussion, they decided to move Maria to a hotel outside of Nashville until the trial. They checked her in under a fictitious name and made sure that the hotel staff knew not to disclose her location to anyone. Lori had fronted the expense with her credit card. She knew that she didn't have much money to work with, but she was determined to do whatever it took to keep Maria safe. As they settled Maria into the hotel, Lori and Shaun made sure to check in on her frequently. They brought her food and other supplies, making sure that she had everything she needed. Despite their efforts, Maria still seemed worried and anxious.

Lori and Shaun knew that they needed to do more to ease Maria's fears. They decided to sit down with her and have a frank conversation about what was going on.

"Maria, we understand that you're scared," Lori said, her voice gentle. "But we want you to know that we're here for you. We're doing everything we can to keep you safe."

Maria looked at Lori and Shaun, her eyes filled with tears. "I don't know what to do," she said. "I'm so scared that they're going to come after me."

Lori reached out and took Maria's hand. "We understand," she said. "But we want you to know that we're not going to let anything happen to you. We're going to keep you safe."

Shaun nodded in agreement. "We've hired a security company to keep an eye on you," he said. "They're professionals, and they know how to handle situations like this."

Maria looked at Lori and Shaun, her expression softening. "Thank you," she said. "I don't know what I'd do without you."

Lori smiled. "We're in this together," she said. "We're going to get through this."

TWENTY-NINE

Lori heard a knock and answered the door to find Mitchell Payne, Shaun's parole officer, waiting outside. Payne had a stern expression and Lori could feel his disapproval the moment she let him into her office. Payne informed Lori that he was there to investigate a report that Shaun had left the state without permission. Lori assured him that Shaun had been working hard for her and had been following all the conditions of his parole. Payne held up a copy of Shaun's hotel receipt from New York. Lori felt her stomach drop. Shaun was placed under arrest as a couple of uniformed officers had accompanied Payne and had stood watch out in the hallway. Kemper Pharmaceuticals wanted to play divide and conquer, not to mention dirty. Lori tried to reason with Payne, explaining that Shaun had only gone to New York on business for their case against Kemper Pharmaceuticals. But Payne was unmoved, citing the strict terms of Shaun's parole.

Lori was filled with a sense of overwhelming guilt as she watched Shaun being led out in handcuffs. She knew that this was all her fault. Her desire to succeed in their case against Kemper Pharmaceuticals had blinded her to the consequences of Shaun leaving the state without permission.

THIRTY

The county jail was a cold, dark place, filled with the sounds of clanging metal and the smell of stale urine. Lori's heart sank as she walked through the metal detector and was led to the visitation area. She could see Shaun on the other side of the glass partition. He looked up and gave her a weak smile as she took a seat on the other side of the phone. "This is all my fault," Lori said, tears streaming down her face. "I should have never let you go to New York."

Shaun shook his head. "It's not your fault. I knew the risks, but I had to do it for the case. I never thought they would catch me." Lori leaned closer to the glass, her heart heavy with guilt and regret. "We have to think strategy now. I think your rights were violated, and I'll do everything I can to get you out of here." You left the state, however, I think your 4th Amendment rights were violated on your visit. I don't think that the laws of Tennessee are applicable in New York. There's also a hospitality law that is supposed to protect your rights to privacy as a guest of the hotel. I don't know how they ascertained a copy of your receipt, but it couldn't have been done with a subpoena. I checked the court records. You might have to spend a night or two in here until I get this figured out. I'll ask for a hearing right away."

THIRTY-ONE

Lori could feel her heart pounding in her chest as she sat in the courtroom, waiting for Judge Emerson Wells to call her brother's case. She couldn't help but feel a sense of dread as she thought about the possibility of Shaun being sent back to jail.

Finally, Wells took the bench, and his bailiff Dax Jenkins called the next case. "22-FH453201, The State of Tennessee versus Shaun Tolliver."

Lori stood up and announced herself as Shaun's defense attorney, while Clayton Purcell, the prosecutor, took his place on the other side of the courtroom.

As the proceedings began, Lori watched as Purcell laid out his case against Shaun, citing his violation of parole by leaving the state without permission. She could feel the judge's eyes on her as he listened to both sides of the argument.

Lori knew that she had to come up with a convincing argument to get Shaun released. She argued that Shaun's trip to New York was for business purposes and that he had simply forgotten to check in with his parole officer, Mitchell Payne.

Judge Wells directed his attention to Purcell, asking if the prosecution had anything additional to add. Purcell shook his head, and Wells turned his gaze to Shaun, asking if he had anything to say for himself.

Shaun stood nervously next to Lori, his eyes downcast as he addressed the judge. "Yes, your honor. I apologize for leaving the state without permission. It was a mistake, and I promise to adhere to the conditions of my parole."

Judge Wells considered Shaun's words for a moment before making his decision. "Typically, the court doesn't allow family members to represent each other. However, given the circumstances and Mr. Tolliver's spotless record while serving his prison time, it's the court's decision to release him this morning."

Lori breathed a sigh of relief as Judge Wells continued to speak. "This is based on Mr. Tolliver's earnest attempt at seeking employment and no report of a crime being committed here or in New York on his visit. I expect that you'll adhere to the conditions of your parole and requests of Mr. Payne here."

Shaun nodded his head, relieved to be released from the courtroom. Dax Jenkins removed the cuffs from Shaun's wrists, and he walked out of the courtroom with his sister by his side.

As they left the courthouse, Lori couldn't help but feel a sense of gratitude for Judge Wells' decision.

THIRTY-TWO

As Lori and Shaun stepped out of the courthouse, they were greeted by a chilly gust of wind that cut through their clothes. The sky was overcast, and the clouds threatened to open up at any moment.

Shaun looked up at the courthouse, a sense of unease settling over him. "Do you think Payne's actions were influenced by a certain someone?" he asked.

Lori nodded her head, a look of determination in her eyes. "I'm sure of it. But we can't let them stop us from getting justice for our client."

Shaun furrowed his brow. "How in the hell did they even know I went to New York?"

Lori adjusted the purse on her shoulder. "Because that's the only other case in the country filed against Kemper. They must have been monitoring us this entire time."

Shaun let out a frustrated sigh. "This is getting ridiculous. We can't let them intimidate us."

Lori nodded her head. "Agreed. That's why I want you to do a little background work on our client Sarah."

Shaun smiled. "I just walked out of there, and now you want me to go back inside?"

Lori smiled back. "At least they'll know you're not going anywhere this time."

Shaun chuckled. "You're terrible."

Lori shook her head, smiling. "Listen, I'm sorry about what happened to you."

Shaun shrugged. "No worries, I'll get mileage out of the next one."

Lori rolled her eyes. "You're impossible."

Shaun took a few steps back up toward the courthouse. "I'll meet you back at the office in a little while. Maybe whoever is following us will tip their hand somehow by me sticking around."

Lori looked up at her brother. "Good idea. We'll talk over lunch. I'll buy the pizza this time. Let's take a break from the turkey sandwiches."

Shaun grinned. "Now you're talking."

As Shaun walked back into the courthouse, Lori couldn't help but feel a sense of unease. She knew that they were up against a powerful adversary, but she was determined to uncover the truth.

THIRTY-THREE

Shaun felt a prickling sensation at the back of his neck as he strolled down the bustling streets of Broadway in downtown Nashville.

He couldn't shake off the feeling that he was being watched. Suddenly, he caught sight of two men dressed in khaki pants and polo shirts, both sporting aviator sunglasses. They were only twenty yards away from him, and their intense gaze made it clear they had their eyes fixed on him.

As he crossed the street, Shaun waited for a horse-drawn carriage to pass by before making his way towards a nearby shop. Once inside, he asked to use the restroom, but instead of exiting through the front door, he slipped out the back. Peering around the corner, he spotted the two men still lurking about, their focus now directed on the shop he had just left.

Shaun took a deep breath and pulled out his cellphone, snapping a few quick photos of the suspicious men. He then made his way towards them, his pace quickening with each step until he stood before them.

"Afternoon, fellas," Shaun said, offering them a smile. "What brings you downtown?"

Both men glared at him, their expressions stony and cold.

Shaun continued, "It's hard to believe that little ole me is the biggest attraction here with all this musical talent around us. Where'd you all get your clothes? The FBI outlet?"

The men's lips tightened in a grim line, their eyes narrowing in suspicion.

"Hold on a minute, fellas," Shaun said, his tone low and steady. "I've seen that look a time or two in the yard while I was in prison. Except this time, we're out in public with plenty of witnesses. Besides, you two don't look like the shanking type anyway. Tell Kemper or Beckham, whichever sent ya to back off. You all be safe now."

With that, Shaun turned on his heel and walked away, whistling a jaunty tune under his breath. As he glanced back over his shoulder, he saw the two men still standing there, their eyes following him as he disappeared into the crowds.

THIRTY-FOUR

Lori's office was filled with the tantalizing aroma of freshly baked pizza from the local Italian restaurant. The restaurant was a small family-owned business, but they were known for their legendary pizza, and Lori and Shaun were indulging in a well-deserved treat after a long day at work.

As they ate, Shaun sifted through some files he had discovered about their client, Sarah. It turned out that Sarah had sued the hospital a few years ago after a C-section delivery, which had resulted in the stillbirth of her baby. To their surprise, Kemper Pharmaceuticals had also been listed as a co-defendant in the case.

"The hospital is one thing," Lori said, taking a bite of pizza, "but Kemper Pharmaceuticals? That's a whole new ball game."

Shaun nodded in agreement, his eyes fixed on the files in front of him. "It gets worse. The attorney representing Sarah dropped out of the case after not being paid, and the case was dismissed soon after."

Lori's eyebrows furrowed in confusion. "That doesn't make sense. Why would the attorney drop out?"

Shaun shrugged, his expression thoughtful. "Could be anything. Maybe the hospital paid off Sarah and the attorney, or maybe Kemper got to them first. Either way, it doesn't bode well for us."

Lori sighed, setting down her slice of pizza. "We need to dig deeper into this. Kemper Pharmaceuticals is a big fish, and we're not exactly swimming in deep waters here."

THIRTY-FIVE

Lori and Shaun stood outside Sarah's door, the chill of the early morning air biting at their noses as they waited for her to answer. After a few minutes of knocking, Sarah finally appeared, looking tired and worn out with dark circles under her eyes. She zipped up her hoodie and invited them inside.

As they entered the living room, Lori and Shaun noticed an empty playpen in the corner. "Baby's asleep finally," Sarah said, sinking onto the couch.

Lori wasted no time. "Why didn't you tell us?" she asked, her tone firm but not unkind.

Sarah looked uncomfortable, shifting her weight from one foot to the other. "I didn't have the money at the time. I'd lost my first child."

Lori paused, watching as Sarah's expression shifted. "The lawsuit you filed against the hospital and Kemper, the one that got dismissed. These are the surprises that could potentially be harmful to your case. They could've already dug through that complaint in their preparation. I'm barely going to have time to review it myself and they have an entire army of attorneys at their disposal."

Sarah put her face in her hands, her breathing unsteady. Lori moved to sit next to her, placing a comforting hand on her back. "Listen, I understand, but you've got to get it together. They could put you on the stand. I can coach you how to answer, but it's still going to be you up there."

"I'm still a bit weak, but I'll manage," Sarah said, her voice trembling.

"We do have some good news," Lori said, changing the subject. "We found an ex-Kemper employee who's willing to testify. Kemper also wanted to propose some sort of settlement."

"How much?" Sarah asked, her eyes wide with anticipation.

"Get this, they wanted to fly us out there to discuss it but never mentioned an amount," Lori said, a smile playing at the corner of her mouth.

"What'd you say?" Sarah asked, leaning forward in her seat.

"I told them not to be late for the deposition," Lori said, grinning.

Sarah laughed, a sound that felt like a release of tension. "That's why I hired you," she said.

"We should probably calculate a figure in case they're serious," Lori said, her tone serious.

"You really think they want to settle?" Sarah asked, her expression wary.

"Kemper is testing the waters at every angle, trying to determine the motivation behind our suit. They've tried to jail Shaun to divide us, they've tried intimidation to see if we'd back off," Lori said, her eyes narrowing. "But we're not going anywhere."

"That's right," Shaun said, his voice low and steady. "We're in this for the long haul."

Sarah looked between them, her expression softening. "Thank you," she said, her voice barely above a whisper. "Thank you for believing in me."

THIRTY-SIX

Shaun leaned against the door frame, watching his sister Lori as she prepared for her first trial. She stood at her desk, her hair pulled back in a tight ponytail, her eyes fixed on the papers in front of her. "You ready?" he asked.

"I think so," Lori said, her voice unsteady.

Shaun raised an eyebrow. "Think?"

Lori took a deep breath, her eyes meeting his. "I'm ready."

"Much better," Shaun said with a smile.

Lori nodded, a flicker of nerves still visible in her expression. "Have you checked on Maria?" she asked, referring to their paralegal.

"She's nervous as hell, but good to go," Shaun said.

"Good," Lori said, taking another deep breath.

As if on cue, the phone rang, the Caller ID displaying the name of the Beckham Law Group, the defense counsel for Kemper Pharmaceuticals. Lori hesitated for a moment before picking up.

"Hello?" she said, her voice calm and composed.

"Lori, it's Gerard Beckham. I wanted to wish you luck on your first trial," Jack's smooth voice came through the receiver.

"Thank you," Lori said, her heart racing.

"I also wanted to propose a settlement," Beckham said, cutting straight to the chase.

Lori felt her pulse quicken as she listened to Beckham's offer. When he finished speaking, she took a deep breath before responding. "We'll have to discuss it as a team," she said, her voice steady.

"Of course," Beckham said, his voice betraying no emotion. "Let me know what you decide."

Lori hung up the phone, her mind racing with the possibilities. She turned to Shaun, her expression serious. "We've got some decisions to make."

THIRTY-SEVEN

Weeks had passed since that early morning visit to Sarah's home. Now, Lori and Shaun sat in a sleek conference room, staring across the table at the legal team from Kemper Pharmaceuticals.

Lori felt a sense of nervous anticipation in her chest. This was it. The moment of truth. The moment when they would find out if all their hard work, all the late nights and long hours, would pay off.

The lead attorney for Kemper spoke first, his voice smooth and confident. "We're prepared to offer a settlement," he said, his eyes meeting Lori's. "It's a fair amount, one that we believe would satisfy your client."

Lori felt a flicker of doubt. Was this really it? Was this the best they could hope for?

She looked over at Shaun, who was sitting calmly beside her, his eyes locked on the legal team.

Lori took a deep breath and spoke. "We appreciate your offer," she said, her voice steady. "But we're not here to settle. We're here to see justice served. And that means going to trial."

There was a moment of tense silence, broken only by the sound of papers rustling as the Kemper team shuffled through their documents.

Finally, the lead attorney spoke again. "Very well," he said, his voice clipped. "We'll see you in court."

And just like that, it was over. The meeting ended, and Lori and Shaun walked out of the conference room, their heads held high.

She spent the next few weeks preparing for the trial, going over her evidence, refining arguments, and practicing the cross-examinations.

And finally, the day of the trial arrived. Lori stood in the courtroom, her heart pounding with anticipation. She looked out over the faces of the jury, wondering what they were thinking, what they were feeling.

As the trial unfolded, Lori felt a sense of exhilaration, of purpose. She was doing what she had always wanted to do, what she had trained for years to do. She was fighting for justice.

And in the end, justice was served. The jury ruled in favor of Sarah, awarding her a substantial sum in damages and holding Kemper Pharmaceuticals accountable for their negligence and failure to warn patients about the risks of their drug, *Eferidine*.

Lori and Shaun left the courtroom, exhausted but elated. They had won. They had made a difference.

As they walked out into the bright sunshine, Lori felt a sense of accomplishment wash over her. She had done it. She had fought the good fight and won.

MORE COLE STEELE BOOKS
BENEATH DEVIL'S LAKE
THE HARVEST SCAR
CRIMSON ROWS
BRETHREN OF LIBERTY
LINE BREAK
CHAMELEON
DEPARTURE
PROSPECTUS
ADMISSION
ENCOUNTER
PERIL
VESPER

Also by Cole Steele

Nashville Justice
Dose of Deception

Roman Lee
Beneath Devil's Lake
Crimson Rows
Brethren of Liberty
Chameleon
Line Break

Willow Darby
Admission
Encounter
Peril
Departure
Prospectus
Vesper
Reticle

Watch for more at https://www.facebook.com/authorColeSteele.

About the Author

Cole Steele is a versatile and talented author residing in the United States. With a vivid imagination and a knack for storytelling, Cole Steele has successfully created two enthralling book stories and a captivating short story series. Cole Steele is deeply grateful to the writers who first ignited the passion for storytelling and provided the inspiration to embark on this creative journey.

With a commitment to crafting immersive worlds and compelling characters, Cole Steele is delighted to offer readers an escape from the mundane and a chance to embark on exhilarating adventures. The warm reception and love for the characters created by Cole Steele have been both rewarding and motivating.

Cole Steele sincerely hopes that you, too, will join the growing community of readers and find solace, excitement, and inspiration in the characters' journeys. So, prepare to dive into the pages and lose yourself in the enthralling worlds that await you.

Read more at https://realcolesteele.wordpress.com/.